P9-CEA-117

# TYAJA

## USES THE

## THINK TEST

# TYAJA USES THE THINK TEST

## A Story About the Power of Words

WRITTEN BY
**LINDA RYDEN**

ILLUSTRATED BY
**SHEARRY MALONE**

TILBURY HOUSE PUBLISHERS, THOMASTON, MAINE

"Let's talk about the power of words," said Ms. Snowden. "Have you ever said something and then right away wished that you could put the words back into your mouth?"

Henry raised his hand. "Oh yeah!" he said. "Yesterday I was so excited about my tooth falling out that I shouted right in the middle of the library! The librarian didn't like that."

Doris said, "Last
night my brother was
bothering me, so I called
him a little worm.

"That made him cry, and then I felt bad too."

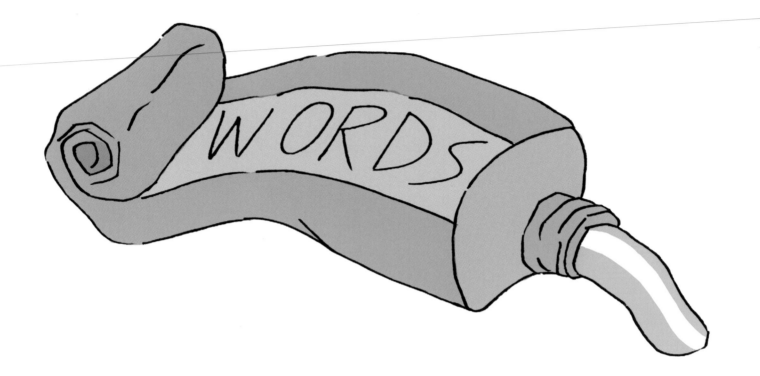

"Remember," said Ms. Snowden, "words are like toothpaste. Once the toothpaste is out of the tube, there's no getting it back in. But I have something that can help."

She wrote the letters T H N K on the board. "What does this look like to you?" she asked.

Delante said, "It looks like THNK. But that's not a word."

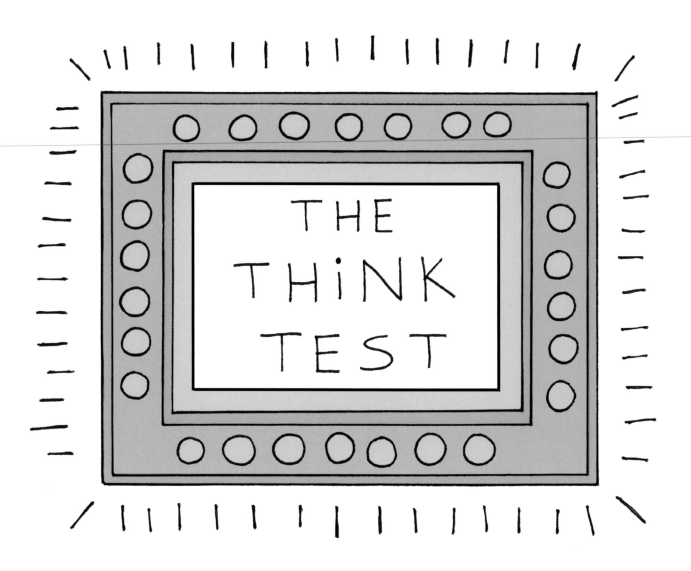

"How about now?" said Ms. Snowden, adding a little i between the H and the N.

Dhariya said, "Now it says 'Think!'"

"That's right!" said Ms. Snowden. "Before you say something, ask yourself if it passes the THiNK Test."

"But what do the letters stand for?" asked Tyaja.

"They stand for four things to think about before you say something," Ms. Snowden answered. "Is it **T**rue? Is it **H**elpful? Is it **N**ecessary? And is it **K**ind? If something doesn't pass the THiNK Test, it's better not to say it."

Delante raised his hand. "I'm confused," he said.
"What does the 'i' stand for?"

Ms. Snowden smiled. "That's simple, Delante.
We need YOU to spell THiNK."

"You mean I'm the 'I' in THiNK?" asked Tyaja.

"That's right! 'I' think before 'I' speak!" said Ms. Snowden.

"Do we have to use the THiNK Test all the time?" asked Sergio. "Do I have to use it before I ask someone to pass the potatoes at dinner?"

"Of course not," said Ms. Snowden. "I think you'll know when to use the THiNK Test. You might hear a little voice inside. You'll see."

Later, during recess, Tyaja saw her friend Rosie on the swings. Rosie had gotten a haircut, and her hair had gone from long to short.

Wow! thought Tyaja. Rosie's hair looks weird. I don't think she should have cut it. I'd better go and tell her.

But as Tyaja headed toward Rosie, she heard a chorus of little voices saying, "Oh, Tyaaaaaajjjjjaaaa . . . ."

"Who's that?" asked Tyaja.

"We're the THiNK Test, Tyaja."

"The THiNK Test?! Come on, is this some kind of joke?"

"No, Tyaja, it's no joke."

Tyaja whirled around, and there, hovering in the air, were four tiny winged people.

The first one swooped forward. "I'm Mr. True," he said, making a little bow. "If you want to be sure the things you say are true, I'm here to help!"

"And I'm Miss Helpful," said the second one. "You have to be careful about how you use your words."

"I'm Mr. Necessary. And Miss Helpful is right, words are powerful."

"I'm Miss Kind," said the fourth tiny person. "You don't want to hurt anyone's feelings, do you?"

"Gee, I guess not," said Tyaja. "But why are you here?
I'm just going to talk with my friend Rosie."

"Yes, we know. You're going to tell her how
you feel about her haircut," said Mr. True.

"And we're here to help you decide if that's a good idea," added Miss Kind.

"Oh, I think it will pass the THiNK Test!" said Tyaja. "Where do we start?"

"Is Rosie's haircut truly awful?" asked Mr. True.

"Yup! It's an awful haircut," said Tyaja.

"We know you believe that," said Mr. True, "but isn't there a difference between an opinion and the truth?"

"Well, it's true that I don't like it," said Tyaja.

"But Rosie might like it a lot. The truth has to be based on facts, and the only fact here is that her hair is shorter than it was. That's why I'm giving a thumbs-down on telling Rosie that her hair looks terrible. It isn't necessarily true!"

Tyaja turned to Miss Helpful. "Don't you think it would *help* Rosie to know that she made a big mistake getting that haircut?"

"Nope," said Miss Helpful. "Once you cut your hair, there isn't much you can do about it except wait for it to grow back. And, like Mr. True said, maybe she likes it. So I'm giving a thumbs-down, too."

"I know *you'll* agree with me," Tyaja said to Mr. Necessary. "I *need* to tell her about her haircut. That makes it necessary, right?"

"Sorry, Tyaja, but this gets a thumbs-down from me, too," said Mr. Necessary. "You may really *want* to tell Rosie how you feel about her haircut, but is that the same thing as *needing* to—like you need food, water, and a safe place to live?"

"No, I guess it's more of a 'want-to' than a 'need-to'," said Tyaja. "But what about video games? Are those a need-to?"

"What do you think?" said Mr. Necessary.

"I know, those are a want, not a need . . . . I was just kidding!"

Then Tyaja asked, "What do *you* think, Miss Kind?"

"I think you know the answer to that one, Tyaja," said Miss Kind. "How would you feel if somebody told you that they thought your haircut was awful?"

Tyaja thought for a moment. "Gee, I guess I didn't really think this through. Telling her would just hurt her feelings, and I don't want to do that. After all, it's what's on the inside that matters, right?"

"Thanks, THiNK Test!"

"You're welcome! Goodbye!"

Tyaja joined Rosie on the swings. "Hi Rosie!" she said.

"Hi Tyaja! I'm glad you came over. My little brother told me that I look like a mop with my new haircut, and it made me feel really bad."

"I'm sorry," said Tyaja. "But who cares what anyone else thinks? Do *you* like your haircut?"

"I really do!" said Rosie.

"Then that's all that matters," said Tyaja.

"You're a great friend, Tyaja!" said Rosie.

# THE THiNK TEST

One of the most important things children can take away from my Peace of Mind classes is how to communicate in a kind and mindful way. When I started teaching the classes more than fifteen years ago, I would feature a quote of the day. I had never heard of talk radio personality and advice-dispenser Bernard Meltzer, but I was really taken with one of his aphorisms. He said, "Before you speak, ask yourself if what you are going to say is true, is kind, is necessary, and is helpful. If the answer is no, maybe what you are about to say should be left unsaid."

When I tried to share this idea with my third-grade classes, the quote seemed too long to be effective. Seeking a way to make it more memorable, I looked at the key words—True, Kind, Necessary, Helpful—and realized that if I reorganized them, they could spell THNK, which is almost "Think," which of course is the point of the quote: to think before we speak. The "I" then stands for "me," as in "**I** think before **I** speak." I decided to call it the THiNK Test and build a game around it. The response from the kids was great, and I've been teaching the THiNK Test ever since.

In class I share the concept and help to define the words—"necessary" is always a bit of a challenge to understand—and then we play the game. I choose four kids to be Mr. True, Miss Helpful, Miss Necessary, and Mr. Kind. I give them name cards to hold, and they stand in front of the class in a line. Then I pose a question. I might say, "THiNK Test, I want to tell my friend that her haircut looks really bad. She should have left her hair the way it was." I tell them that I'm checking with them before I talk to my friend, and I start by asking Mr. True, "Isn't it true that it's a terrible haircut?" This always leads to a lively discussion about the difference between fact and opinion—something we adults need to be thinking more about these days. Then I ask Miss Helpful, Miss Necessary, and Mr. Kind for their opinions, after which the team lets me know if what I want to say passes the THiNK Test.

The kids love this game, and we usually do several rounds. Questions might include: "I want to tell my friend that his zipper is down"; "I want to tell my friend that the movie she wants to watch is babyish"; or "I want to tell my friend that I heard that so-and-so has a crush on her." The THiNK Test gives my students a chance to grapple with ethical questions and think for themselves.

I wrote *Tyaja Uses the THiNK Test* to spread this message of mindful communication. It is one example of mindfulness practice, something that serves children well as they get older and are confronted with more difficult choices.

Another mindfulness practice, *Take Five Breathing*, is a great way for kids to calm down when they get angry or upset and to take a pause before speaking or acting. In Take Five Breathing, you simply trace your hand onto a sheet of paper. As you trace up your thumb you breathe in, and as you trace down you breathe out. You continue tracing and breathing until you have traced all the fingers on one hand. Repeat on the other hand for a little extra calmness!

For more resources, please visit the Peace of Mind website at: https://TeachPeaceofMind.org.

Tilbury House Publishers
12 Starr Street
Thomaston, Maine 04861
800-582-1899 • www.tilburyhouse.com

Text © 2019 by Peace of Mind
Illustrations © 2019 by Shearry Malone

Hardcover ISBN 978-0-88448-735-7
eBook ISBN 978-0-88448-737-1

First hardcover printing June 2019

15 16 17 18 19 20 XXX 10 9 8 7 6 5 4 3 2 1

Library of Congress Control Number: 2019939488

Designed by Frame25 Productions
Printed in Korea

☑ TRUE
☑ HELPFUL
☑ NECESSARY
☑ KIND

To my sister Tricia—the truest, most helpful, most necessary, and kindest person I've ever known.
—LR

LINDA RYDEN is the full-time Peace Teacher at Lafayette Elementary School, a public school in Washington, DC, where she teaches weekly 45-minute classes to more than 600 children. She is also the creator of the Peace of Mind program and curriculum series, which includes *Peace of Mind: Core Curriculum for Grades 1 and 2* and *Peace of Mind: Core Curriculum for Grades 3-5*. Her work has been recognized in the *Washington Post* and the *Huffington Post*, and her program has been featured on local CBS, ABC and Fox5 news stations. Linda's books include *Rosie's Brain*, which uses a humorous story to introduce elementary school students to mindfulness skills. She is also the author of *Henry Is Kind* and *Sergio Sees the Good*. Linda lives in Washington, DC with her husband, their two children, and their dog Phoebe.

SHEARRY MALONE studied art at Lipscomb University in Nashville. She is the illustrator of the *Absolutely Alfie* books, a spinoff from the *EllRay* Jakes series. In *Henry Is Kind, Sergio Sees the Good,* and *Tyaja Uses the THiNK Test,* Shearry's loose, quirky illustrations make Henry, Sergio, Tyaja, and their pals as universally appealing as the kids in Charlie Brown's world.